dante in the laundrette

dante in the laundrette

sean burn

Published 2012 by
Smokestack Books
PO Box 408, Middlesbrough TS5 6WA
e-mail: info@smokestack-books.co.uk
www.smokestack-books.co.uk

dante in the laundrette
sean burn
Cover image: sean burn
Author photograph: ovada

Printed by
EPW Print & Design Ltd

Middlesbrough
moving forward

ISBN 978-0-9568144-8-7

Smokestack Books is
represented by Inpress Ltd
www.inpressbooks.co.uk

this book is dedicated to miki z

Acknowledgements are due to the editors of the following publications where some of these poems were first published: *at last, borderlines, broken fiddle, the coffee house, the delinquent, dreamcatcher, echo room yearbook, fire, glass house, jones av (canada), the journal, links, neon highway, nightingale, northwords, papillon, pennine ink, presence, purple patch, rain dog, red herring, the reator, rising, seam, sepia, skald, the slacker, smiths knoll, smoke, snapshots, splizz, staples, tangled hair, terrible work, time haiku, transparent words, upstart, the yellow crane; online at aabyes baby, great works, ism (seattle), onesixty, otoliths, transparent words, veer;* also the following anthologies: *left to write, poetry in motion and paternoster* (potsdam).

iamnot was first published as a broadsheet/exhibition catalogue for inside out (buddle arts), *mind the reality gap* was first published on the tyne and wear metro, pack of cards (aberdeen libraries) and poems on the buses, london. *outstaring* was part of an installation with andrew hardie shown in huddersfield, middlesbrough, york and newcastle in 1999 and 2000. *leery* was first published as a pamphlet by inkstone and received a northern arts writers award in 1997. *eyes of honey* and *this tumbled stone* have been made into short poetry films and screened in belfast, cologne, leeds, middlesbrough, newcastle and yerevan. *symphony of ravens* was commissioned as part of *odins glow*, an outdoor celebration in october 2009 for 10,000 visitors over 4 nights under an illuminated roseberry topping on the north york moors. an early version of *honeysuckled* was commissioned by the new word order and performed there and at the hydrogen jukebox alongside a soundmap and cut-up visuals.

contents

dante in the laundrette

down on me

she plays those tapes he left behind
etta james and janis joplin   loves singing

though mam says *you gotta work*   she
gets there late   short-changes twats

leaves early   saturday   telling insecurity
cameras to fuck off   she empties the till

fucks off   and now outside the chippy   belting
to her mates   *you gotta gettit while you can*

valentine's day mascara

even the godsquads gobsmacked   stop praying
and kneel before quartet of drum and bass
and guitar and sax basting this place
day racing to some kinda turbocharged tango

fingers snap like crazy calypsoing christs
now arms outstretched as they forgive
sporty spicy and jailbaity in identikit adidas
who cant help moaning and swaying to all that jazz

valentines day mascara runs and the whole
caboodle hopscotch across cracks
as a great cry goes up from saint james park
someone scores   or misses

an evening in the weimar republic

cables sinuosity flexes   curves
to   whip-hand tight over mike as we
underclass raise glasses through
smokechoke to marianne faithfull
playing the lemon tree like
a battered grand   hitting all
our kinked keys   major   minor
underground   white and black and white
strike shades of blue   crush
of accidentals passing through
she's belting twentieth century blues
so late on theres no going back

stony vocals chiselling edges
off granite city   her flirt and and tease
teaching a lechers history
i know about the seven deadly sins
and eight nine ten in her scandal school
we bruise easy as fermenting fruit
in case of emergency break
and wineglasses crack underfoot

after   to stumble out   night-blind
through streets slippy with haar
her underground pulse still swinging
still driving   still fucking   still desired

mayday

milk crate
taking weight
he hunkers down
to harmonica
bendingscraping
stretching realities
in and outta
footsteptime

his 13 stitches
and a scab
where *love*
was tattooed
mesmerise
this kid in
leathers into
falling off heels
just when
kevlar cops
come move
'em on

history lessens

in uniform nike
dark as tyne
schools out
and hoarding their
sweets dreams
like theres no
tomorrows
in cartoon-town
laugh as dodgy photos
of ashley
are passed around
and fagpacks
in mayfair blue
tumbleweed
through wallsend
and metros
pass in midair
lording it over
thicksteak
fishcakes
charity shops
and futures
in the balance
of 12 year olds
hanging off metros
shouting *i-lu-uv-yu*
without knowing
its coin

          survivors
trainsurfing curve
of possibilities
one more stop
down the line

eyes of honey

smiles in quayside sun
wild ringlets of laughter
dribbling down child-face
tasting of honey
from eyes of honey
tears of such joy
she shakes calypso
tearing us from tide

decades past
holding hands
with little-sis
catching folks between
and laughing
laughing up whole shoals
this net of flesh-meshed
shimmying up/down
and us eyed-wide
brilliant in innocence

16/10

we've just been three hours on the camino real
kilroy and me and tennessee williams
and now i'm crying by the monument
as window undressers roll home
and someone walks past shouting
and someone flicks a lighter
although they don't smoke
and someone panhandles
and i'm guilty of the apple muffin
warming my pockets
knowing they need food
and knowing the booze will win
wait until she's gone and i eat it quickly
fingers all sticky   crumbs become evidence
though all i hear is *america here is thy son*
and all anyone else hears are cries of *chronicle* and seagulls
and in the pizza express they don't hear that
only see mouths opening like so many toppings
and streetlights are gold against honeyed sandstone
and it chimes 5:30   5:45   6 o'clock
and this guy sits down   headphones large as tennessee
all ticking and clicking and buzzing and aching
until he hits the rewind   and a white stick
hits the chewing gum and no-one gives a hand
and i'm on dothiepin   and i'm debating
chucking my dole on tequila or scotch
and a bouncer walks past all aftershave and no neck
and his carrier bag busts and he whispers *oh fuck*
looks round guilty to see if others heard
as sirens a semitone out and half a beat out
wail past without stopping
and headphones does a runner
past f.c.u.k. which is opening soon
and lynsey and d.c and l.a was here
and kilroy came saw and was conquered
and *america here is thy son*
but the eyes-down crowd all search for small change

and i listen to their symphonies of feet
down grey streets to the river to the sea
and a wean tugs his father who chills
to two men trading licks on a single 99
and kilroy rises   says he is lost   and i am too
and the disorientate ask for directions
to the *demolition in progress*
where a flowerseller packs up her stock
and a woman passes arm round her daughter
and another mother passes holding hands with her son
and i wish i could ask what all this feels like
cos i don't know and neither does kilroy
and no-one asks *why you crying*
though i wait for raised hands
and *stop crying* but i cant
and as 6:30 sounds
they're taking it out on kilroy
on his gold boxing gloves

they're chanting *englandamerica here is thy son*
and the clarinet starts on gershwin in tyneside
and i'm having difficulty reading the writing
and kilroy holds out his hand says *i was sincere*
to the camera flashing weegee in newcastle
in pools of blood no even making front pages
and security checks out two girls passing arm-in-arming
and its too cold for short short skirts
and i'm cold in a world of another's making
where a drunk bellows and kilroy follows
the homeless taking turns
combing their hair
as valpolicella clots
and the temperature drops
and the bouncer returns
holding hands with his lover
beneath anarchies of starlings patching the sky
still i hear the cry *here is thy son*
and a guy lets his bouquet slip
to the feet of this platinum bombshell
cheered on by toon-army

into cutting up biblethumpers
skirt rides up   reveals the unmistakable
tranny with fucking attitude
and none of 'em knows which way to take it
and a girl and her da bite into whoppers
steam rising off week old cattle
and snakeboarders domino the street
and someone adjusts their laces
pulls on their bonnet
asks if i'm from the church
asks if i'm the preacher

and i laugh out loud *here is thy son*

late night shopping

people oscillate
jostle the crowded street

breath biting lung
begins this november dusk

scarves   insecurity
late night shopping

church spire sharp   clock still
an hour fast   floodlit features

this city contains
more colours than grey

witness pink sky heal
encroaching wound of night

graveyard

i   silver birches

silver birches
mossed in repeat
seep of guttered rain

hangout for sisters
whose moonshine limbs
rave   vogue   tempt

where syringes drop
deals are done

ii   crows

gang of hooded bullies
pickpocket the peace

turn over trash
gatecrash uniformed
lunch of office workers

anarchic to the last
their raku winging it
through vermilion skies

iii   agave

graffiti tears flesh

slow bullet
aimed across
our wounded
century

stopped within
agaves deep
blades of green
which conduct

deserts red coda

this tumbled stone

cormorant
at anchor
inscribes itself
on bridge-foot
slick as oil
spelling s for storm
rupture/d
before

herons great flags of
raggedy not-so-new print
newburn to ouseburn
in dispirited priestly grey
record signings
so much ash blown
forlornly down tyne

kittiwakes, kittiwoken
croaks, crick-crack
broke yr etceteras
egalitarian kittiwake this
shat on all and sundry
shat on earl grey
shat on girls aloud
shat on nick brown
scavenging the new
classless society
- we are all panini now

starlings explode
orange to green
iridescent improbable
catherine-wheeling
neat optical illusions
like blood turning
under new moon

wren stumbles through
the weathered boneyard
a thumbful of feathers
small liturgies
tying up this tumbled stone

iamnot

that one a.m. jazz   jazz kissing   the echo
from roland kirks great fat lips wailing as
he was by then keeping on blowing to the second
stroke after midnight fatal blown ragged
through my balcony palace two floors up all the
concrete you can dream cruddas park
turning heads from lad on lad giving tongue
and does it surprise does it my latest love
is no a man

                              and still *petite fleure* yaps
kisses spit into sax   harmonica   whistles
flute   taking the beat from morello lips
wrapped hard round brass round silver
round sliver horns   your lips bite the dark and all
this while toyshop sounds willing us honey
before unleashing the swarm

                                        cruddas park rising
above sodium lighting the gasdoesntworks
the redheugh bridge   vickers rolling tanks
out one end of scotswood road the other
towards the arena the petty car thieves
the windscreen spray   so many diamonds
tripping pavements with moonlight   and as the
city breathes   and as the jazzblind prophet
walks   talks   breathes through my lovers stereo
and as the freedomjazz prophet breathes again
i breathe believe rhythms of the city bus taxi
metro tyres brakes rubber glass grass bricks
rhythms of the espresso night percolating my
veins and i believe too   i too believe a twelve
bar twisted passiondance   fucking with you
oh baby i'm fucking with you

                              roland kirk still through stereo
pulling out horn to accompany the travelling
weeping laughing crying along with the wheels the
engines the cockpit voices   and now the kiss of silver
spinning on her c.d. an alternative record of history
alternate takes to kiss babies dogs headlies
mistresses sucking up tabloid moralities
winning the last erection and by and by tory turned
tony and spraycans marking b.n.p. are back again
and belsen's a bus stop on park road according
to these same flowerfairies and i'm semtext
dreaming fat bisexual poetry as revolt as
revolution as a mark as a means of raising
a busted hand a pierced eyebrow a ...
as way of saying of throwing down my way of
agreeing *we all are driven by an invisible whip*
i'm driven the city driven jazz driven jazz
driving i'm driving these words outta here

outta the city outta the way driven leatherwards
dickpierced tonguepierced outta the concrete hitting
speed limits hitting higher no hitting the brake
the brakes coming up trumps

twisted blade of sax opening face
too hard too fucking hard   a sort-of
off-white silver gay grey moving on
and up through clots of red viscera

another flowernazi tubthumped out

remembrance sunday

magpie
                its beak
trapped inside last nights
can of mcewans

unable to break free
to fly away

dante in the laundrette

its the third circle   where it rains
forever   malign   cold and heavy
it never eases   it never changes
like every place i've been moved on from
and i'm reading dante in the laundrette
fine on this overdue translation racks up
drums of washing speed or slow
as hub of heat battles squalls of hail
which part and sting and slant silver birch
and gulls are so many carrier bags
spewed feral on wind and hurled through my
kingdom   all towerblocks and tenements

churchless towers huddle in conspiracy
outsized car stereos for the taking   tuned
permanently to uneasy listening   by now
i'm reading *our minds will go completely null*
as badly worn smalls mediums larges spin
the polycotton mix no longer washing
just like his vowels at the jobless centre
youth asks for a light   says obsessively
i've seen yer seen yer i've seen yer
as security guards enter to empty machines
realise i'm no threat and bid *how ya doin?*
pull up my sleeves and bare slashed wrists

i've no seen terror-wrist acts bad as they
penny for halloween eh   this dull thud
of fireworks should be three weeks away
but the flash of blue and thump of powder
is undeniable   *why must you kick*
against the pricks   why even ask
where memory is lost and dreams the first
things stolen i seek redemption through words
you ask for miracles   they're delivering
oxygen to the 16th floor as i turn
water into urine   go back to your washing
cleanse stain on your sheets   cycles done

24/12

pulsing to the bigg markets disco beating
a butcher heaves past with bleach as
wannabes swig scrumpy   crush tinnies
in the gloom   big issues having a hard time
pushing christmas specials this month of blue
green pink yellow red blue lights on the blink
as strangers snog like long lost friends
and puffa-jacketed ambassadors
push the latest slot deals to kids
who stomp their freebie balloons
amid this hungerford on helium
body hits deck   pretends he is drunk
and fishing pizza from bins   veins
his solzhenitsyn beard with mozzarella

and they're mopping down boomroom steps
sweeping out the t.s.b. and petitioning our sex shop
with closure as *its the first thing tourists see*
and lipstick lasses freeze their tits off queuing
for speedbanks going down   *fightfightfight*
fightfight   we got a regular xmas party
with booze and bruisers and praying for strippers
and days white as the driven cocaine
earl greys monumentally pissed off
looking down on his gunmetal town   until
this woman scatters hemp from her liberty
carrier-bag and rolling stones spill out of doorways
blinded by rainbows and faces in windows
d'ya dream at night   i doubt it

somewhere milometers are hymning us toward the next set of zeros

and northumberland streets snowing
the wet kiss of expectation
of black and white movie
all silvers down to a soft shoe shuffle
us in slow motion   freeze frame
in the now   we are   all your kids
film extras forgetting ourselves
mouthing wide the great soft flakes
like the song of the ice cream van
on this the coldest day
its sheer unexpectedness
summoning us back down years

5/1

sourmash reels
through greenmarket
and butchers red
topside and silverside
trotters and black pudding
kissing and wishing us all
happy new year
though he's five days out

mcenemy

there's no escapin me always kennin where you live
the chill in your head freezin your redstuff over and over
comin back for your sirloin, topside, ribs and trotters, more

shuttit mcenemy

        and six guards haul dole generations molotov from dock
to serve five year though we always knew he'd be out before
weans six and seven while *wifie*, i gave the eight longest of my life

leaves stick like shit underfoot
trick or treating kids dressed as devils   witches   ghouls
cheap masks asking uncertainly for money

hoodie-crow knifes my estate on this day of grey and gold
looking out and onto a double rainbow - the first burning
our ashen sky while the seconds a more distant memory

mcenemy sent down
and i'm halfway
through blue-black
of nightfall

headphones ache
cemetery songs
bruising blues
mourning our loss

beyond bridge where
only dream remains
bones sharp
to windblade

and a submerging
in memory of
slab surrenders
to the horizontal

seeing my name *kim*
cut into its stone i grab weans
and race for the future
as past takes hold again

no close in my family   they drifted
i drifted further   ending beside pub
whose the bins are emptied by gulls
fight-fucking   snowballs hurled with grit

                    m   s
                      a   c
                        n a
                        i

        s
        c
      i
    m
    i
      t
        a
          r
            i
              n g

another bloody sunset where i unscrewed
wedding ring   hurling the hoop against
fingers of rock   white thunder rubbing salt
into wound of this outstretched hand
are tears eroding our land

kelp snares and welts a steady beat
where earlier we cartwheeled through
bleached crab-backs like torn fingernails
then upturned   frail boats putting to sea
and a heron lands   raggedy newspaper

blowing down foreshore   yesterdays news
as i was   but now i long for tomorrow
and though others let their weans walk home
alone i'm scared mcenemy'll rip 'em
from the light of me turn 'em to the dark

bosie weans as they gabble together
on days schooling   holding up
treasures of their making   wish i could
enjoy clays roundness again
apple no-ones gonna eat   *and mam*
the head asked us about home

i says you's the best but he was
only interested in da so i says
he's locked up but he cant hear
right   thought i sweared f word
they laughed loud as he turned red

mcenemy enters and breaks again

- seen new lass?
kim   sommat scottish
/ haven't seen hubbie
if she is?
/ mebbe did away with him
/ really   shouldn't say
such terrible
/ betcha he left
for another woman
/ dreadful bringin
young-uns up
alone when he's
gallivantin off

/ make yourself at home
/ we're not the city
/ all one happy family
/ know everyone's name
/ nothin hidden
but they don't ken
secret of me slipping
his chokechain
praying he never
finds   until one stills
her hand on mine
saying *i'm jeannie*
and winks at me

in house alone
so i picks up phone
then stares   remembers
there's no-one to dial
no even 999 anymore
only calls i get are

double-glazing cheap
to council flat
or cable when we cant
afford licence and all those ads
everyone's gottit mam
can-we-can-we pleeease

jumping outta skin
as the plastic voice shouts
though no-one answers
my whispered *whose there?*
1471 saying caller
withheld number again

stomach jitterbugging
until jeannie knocks on door
asks me for coffee
take her arm pleading
get me out before i'm
disconnected permanently

never close when we was together
just drifting to fucking as you do
and onto weans   being learnt to forgive
when all that fills dreams is

ken i yelled these last twelve months
and battered seven shades of shite from you
but doll darlin quine its fourteenth feb
and i've declared truce for the day

in no woman's land   hell i'll even say
luv you these 24 hours from reality
so doll darlin quine   here's your bottle
cheap and rosy   happy bloody valentine

weans replay high-lights
of last nights pray-per-view fight
for which he wrote rules and he refereed
weaving home like footballer

though only league is his own
kenning he's gonna score
i'm late-tackled   hacked down
no-one daring show red card

as whisky in hand he towers over
glowering pulls out *whorebasher*
and sticks me   and sticks me
bottle at throat only this time its broke

and glassing me neck and a & e
reckons i was lucky to last
he's dragged off shouting *mangy cur*
i'll always be your mcenemy

tell all this to jeannie
over three too many
bottles of lambrini
weans cosied up
in midnight bed
she pulls me towards her
and then she pulls
doing stuff i never
thought possible
until we surface
for breath and laugh

still in lust
the next night
and her mam
tucking our weans
up tight we hits
pink triangle
the nearest city
where she swings
all ways
such a sight
for my sore eyes

fridaysaturday
night is
happy hour
on hour here
in the fleshgarden
where i bend
to salt 'n' vinegary
tarmac   pick up
carnation still
warm and pink
as her cunt

mcenemy and me met in another city
beside timetables i says *excuse me* too loud

then stop as he stares at my belly pale as frost
and we tango through traffic to far sides of the street

next day he pays for daisy-chain round ankle
devil in red boxing gloves on left shoulder

where my woman now kisses   nothing was amiss
until he breaks mirror over me head looks down and laughs

from bad to worse as i catch him on metro looking at
breast enlargement posters again   imagining his-self

two sizes smaller and wearing my skin
at last one day i'm scrambling for change

two hearts in a co-op bag as my man goes hungry
and weans cry like saxophones in the night

jeannie that's how it was   now hold me tight

mcenemys no into ceasefires
i'm on dothiepin hydrochloride

so sedated busting blisterpack
and what day we on anyway

gotta get it in your system
gotta let it take effect

seventy five milligrams
two each night   avoid alcohol

avoid driving   i'm a 45 at 33 r.p.m.
i'm a poorly dubbed film

the good   the bad   the fucking ugly
thinking outta sync

i'm photo in long exposure
still round ghosted cities turning

streetlights are birthday candles which i blow
make my wish as rain blurs the ac/dc of night-city
largactyl-dreaming of first electric chair in this place

cross my fingers and he rounds corner from burgerking
sweating quarterpounders   my fat n greasy slips down wet
steps
and into statue which has lost both my hands

strapped to the pulsing throne we ride and writhe
alive in shock as i point to his fallen meat
and scream   *now d'ya want fries with that?*

wean chases gaudy rag held high on wind and then returned
slow-whip kite-tail loops lazy kissing ground   small footsteps

telling where she has been but no where she is headed
as jeannie struggles and his circle of rope tightens my neck

curlews pibroch below hills-crest where two nations collided
and wind hurls fist full of shrieking feathers through me

deepening sky   rooks laugh through storm   i cry
into chill of mcenemy hunting me down

bonfire nights early this year
sky rioting as ribs of my lasses car

are barbecued by this guy
bought in by mcenemy to burn us good

fist-stuffed with twenties for his pains
notes crisp as gunpowder

eyes blue as petrol   deep as hate
never missing a beat

my enemy's calling card
gallows humour burning outta control

hello in waiting rooms when goodbye would be more like
lords snorting inheritance away - lady blahblah's
vomiting and gin - beating ex-royals-wives -

and do try winning our coverstars fabulous frock
you'll hardly notice the stains   queuing for help
though best these places do is a nice cuppa

to the stressed depressed battered suicidal - *see he's*
left you with both arms in plaster again, i'll be mum
receptionists hymn   *hope there's not too much sugar*

and i'm supposed to wash down my happy tablets
with a dose of take-it-easy
i'll put you down for follow up on monday ok

is there anyone with whom you could stay?
just put me down for bloody coffin, five foot nothing
and two for my weans   *police can advise on your safety*

if he does harass in any way   but bizzies are
bastards as gave mcenemy my new address
cos the wanker in a wig judged psychofather

family man and my weans needing his role model
eyes blow up storm as she hands me appointment card
with their number on when its mine that's up

cos mcenemys out on good behaviour
and a man of his word
does no-one on this lump of rock give a fuck

as she holds door open
and with nowhere else to go
i walk out alone to face my enemy

hard keeping still enough to read
i'm the flame that never blows out
ripped and pasted through letterbox
my hand cut on his hate-mail   doublecheck
deadlocks though mcenemy unpicks everything
save my deathsentence and the nearest police
seven miles away and unmanned this time of day

trying no to do my nut at weans
until jeannie takes us for last walk
below grit cliffs blunted by wind-whip
bowed pink head of thrift
on ledge this border country
inky sea and snowstorm merge
how to make my peace?

wedge this strip of rowan
to thorns of black rock
take salt-sucked plastic
flayed by wind and fresh off the tide

hang these bare branches
with twist-fruit for my falling body
though who'll conduct this requiem?

walk home with jeannie's hands round me
and rain bows farewell to the al
a spectrum taking flight
bridge hurled to infinity

weans cling round my neck in goodbye
tell 'em *be good*   tell 'em no to cry
and now without place to hide i'm writing
all this down before

                hoodies blades of black
slice this savage season
closer than petals
shadow knifes fast-grieving

distant cities glow

dark rocks
and half way below

herring gull
razorbill
kittiwake
puffin
fulmar
gannet
shag

parliament
in session
as
fathom
on fathom
of sheer
rock
dives
toward
oiled sea

waves
exploding
hitlists

snipe point
surf whispering
through mist

      barbwire sings
in the wind
- and a solitary curlew

           oystercatchers
           off waren mill
           gurgling through haar

                    moon shines
                    through slats of blind
                    drunks sing outside

              among concretes
              the unexpected perfume
              of honeysuckle

dunes are tattoos snaking round arm of the north sea

              night falls
              - lights going out
              one by one

moor burns
white feather drifting
through bracken

foxgloves
        purple spike
quickening the heart

        springtime bracken
     unfurls
  even
the rock

          cool morning grey swell
escorted by cormorants
we land on inner farne

     black rock white lighthouse
     streaks of birdshite
     stain inner farnes cliff

inky thumb print
on blank page of this morning
crows in snow
        - belford moor

    marramgrass
cementing
land with sea

poppy scythed from verge of the a1
gladrags cast aside

white bell of campion closing

fuck all to do except fuck
tidesline is condoms

journeys end

a single footprint
on goswick sands

gob, aye

i

howling blue, howling black, gobs vowels
aquaplane *why yer forsakin me?*

waking to hell-salt on tongue - whose, he don't know
so very much down this cursed town an
twinned with nowhereville dontcha?

gob only knows the coal dark as his veins
bus-shelter mary nursing gods foetus of night-before
knows a firemans hose when he sees one

gobby boots, gobby clothes, gobby eyes - *yer states of dis*
-grace an last clocks home, aye thats the drop on me

ii

hanging out priestpopple bus station
waiting cashcow through
guys been let out that morning
an yet to be placed on the register

easy gobbo, jeans half-mast
his christ-grin, yer couldn't make it up
pasties are only 1:59 fer three an
the wentworth bogs new-painted

iii

wants the last plastic mechagodzilla
each an every large lollipop
to be drunk on shearer united
draped in department store
widows, the *fantasie* collection
lavenders an blues

gob creams the balance
ballet of fag an iron bru
off balance, over-warmed
through an through
cough-cough an
whats in it fer me eh?
whats in it fer me?

new labour already ending
his 13 years unlucky
fer some curfews an
parental bonds an
first time was easy
poverty trap they say
an the sins of fathers
growing each an every day

iv

gob-jobs off-of platform one though more like teases, an no
out on the edge *northern spirit* thundering past, but between
engine room an rim of public disinformation, locked most
days, kinda appropriate really, on the road an off the rails
between a rock an etcetera

V

already halfway to a bacon sarnie
whisky-tin upstairs where gob lives
roll of notes rustling from back-pockets
the three tenners - only other song he needs

vi

nasturtium happy days
knock-ankle adidas ways
fingerless gloves an now
gobs stroking the photo
going, going - thumbprints
where bluebell eyes should-of

us wee mouth-hawks
how the hunted fox feels
yr bitin our necks no fer
meat but the sheer bloody
hell ma bird yer was an only
twelve when hunted down

vii

stampede of benson an hedges twist an
heineken pissing it to the new blue floor
smirnoff spins the bottle an the new doors
already peeled into a map of bonnie an clyde

gobs on his knees -sweet-jesusing - shirt hung
outback his gap an c.c.t.v. blind to that far corner
glad to at last spill his fools gold, guts heaving

viii

stop an go in force
can you help with our murder
posters on all approaches
even the ex-bunker
possible nuke attack
an now flattened fer a new
outta retail experience
guardian abandoned at station
folds to letters to the editor
on *le vice anglais*
prudhoe-wylam-riding mill
wakes until the pool table
shuttit, i'm tryin to score

symphony of ravens

prologue

root, bark, leaf - yggdrasil the guardian tree branching out and
  across many worlds.
root, bark, leaf - yggdrasil's early days and late nights journeying
  this multiverse.
root, bark, leaf - yggdrasil our guardian tree carving where
  past-present-futures collide

1

moors above, smokemonster below and my longings for
beyond. teessides street-lights, gasflares, bonfires - who in
their solitude didn't rhyme the night-sky alight? yet each
morning made anew - sun-warp, leaf-bright, web-dew.
pulling keys off ash-trees - those single-winged seeds - and
pickling the greenest, not everything is syrup as i have learnt.
a friend brings rowan jelly, hold that up against sun-warp,
leaf-bright, web-dew and you will be transported too. still
points in the tippings of child-destiny, aye. cleveland moors
above, smokemonster below, and my longing for beyond

2

this mazer, this one who amazes, who amazes me still, spent
their childhood in a hedge. clambering years inside that great
knotted length. read in their eyes the shapeshift-imagined back
and rooting. of course, that was now and this is then - how
time circles, times circling yes, and not as clockface, rather the
roll-and-tumble raven in long-flight, cascading ever-game
thermals, that feather-river of all. how in any hundred foot of
hedge each plant found means a hundred years of life.
hawthorn, blackthorn, beech, sweet-briar, dog rose, holly,
bramble, rowan, honeysuckle and hop and that great woven
wall goes right back to the writing down of north myths.
smokemonster's hedge was one species - municipal, right-
angled, evergreen. once, this wee blob pink at me feet. had i
stepped in bubblegum? then blob-pink starts scrattling: beak
wider than the imagined future. i place that tiny croak back to
its nest, a rune only time will read

3

above roseberry topping, clouds were longboats, dragons,
lungs. and up ahead this weather-worn, this beech-nut, this
gargoyle, words slow as volcano.
- you placed that fallen fledgeling back to nest.
- howdya?
- one wish.
-but howdya?
- this is about you no me. one wish now, what would it be?
- a story then.
- aah, a dreamer. they say two ravens - hugin and munin,
thought and memory - sit one to each my shoulders. truth
is, i was called to their flight. what i have learnt is you must
write your own story. lonely is it no? roots like iron, but
always looking to blossom, even in midwinter. for you a joke
: why do bees strike? for more honey and shorter working
flowers!
i look into a great whorled pool, forged and furrowed where
his eye should. the haar swallows moors around while a pair
of ravens caa--caak caa--caak in warp and weft

4

raven-we above all your cloud appreciation societies, catch-
me-if-you-can out of asia, bridging greenland to america - our
winged speak, how our wings speak. an unkindness of ravens
- no - call us a kindliness rather! didn't we give away stars,
water and fire, aye, when the whole of creation hung from
cruel eagles lodge and you cowered before. not raven! we
snatched creation up, loop-outlooping the chase, finding just
where to hang up the stars; out-out-tumbling the chase until
exactly where to let flow and fall all waters of this world;
wing-whistle-outwit and ... only firebrand in beak and don't
laugh no, our feathers singed from that day on, raven-we
dropping firebrand down among rock. how you learnt to
strike two stones, sparks firing, and off-and-outing. and now?
high above your cacophony, our brothers/sisters wingclipped
in london tower, they call out free-free, free us, free!

5

that long-ago mead of climbing out and above and what i
have seen in the clouds since. odin giving an eye to drink
from that wisdom well, hanging nine days from yggdrasil so
his mind could fill with poetry, and still we search for that
midwinter garden in full blossom. now fix to memory,
völuspá. vö-lus-pá! this wise-woman's runes and ruins, dust
and dusk of a thousand years, back when volcanoes spat the
skies dark and the rising sea threatened to wash all away

6

waters rising, mountains burning, summer after summer the
sunshine black, do you see? white mud spattering brown
leaves of yggdrasil, do you see yet, do you see? beaks
trembling with red soot, words break, their long-line sundered,
do you see? at last moon-dark, earth-sink, tremble-star.
moon-dark, earth-sink, tremble-star. is this the void? no. that
wise-woman vö-lus-pá clings with iron roots, seeing beyond.
seize beyond. we may yet break this leash. break this leash!
arise a second time, earth from ocean, and beautifully green.
see? see! *earth from ocean, a second time, and beautifully green*

epilogue

leaf - bark - root : - this guardian tree of yggdrasil.   how
those ravens thought and memory rebuild their nest, rebuild
their nest, rebuild, times circlings. so take a sapling, a
youngling, a wildling, allow their branching out and across
multiverses, carving where past-present-futures collide

never sleep with anyone who has more
scars than you

child of the mirrorglass
reflecting white stone towers
whitestone towering against grey sky
how much else is needed?
how much else is?

look, wait, ogle road, ogle street
snatch at high-heels, through-traffic
car stereos underpassing
the clack of skateboards skinny
of gulls above and the cash machine below
the most-bell of england, record this

diesel, mercedes, chipper
drum towers, bladderwrack
no appointment necessary just call
chateau (of) pain
models needed
for sunday roast
pickets and pursers
carve within
just add water
just add laughter
to the skin just add
a sweet sweet dash of

offduty police, nasty scars those, i'm calling for back-up / do / state
number, state unit number

the scuff of leaf piercing
and raindrops keep
heels and reels
drilling nights
centre now closed
autumn croci

psilocybin
20% weightloss
a crow eating fried bread
self-reliance of the working man, reconstructed 1971

bump and hustle
naked in court
blues-soul espressos
all deliveries to rear of
get a good gut feeling
luxury hand service
whitestone etceteras
against grey sky
even tv aerials are masts
how much else?

join pilgrims on the dock	wilhelmsen	pink hussy on black
pilgrims on the dock	wallenius	s.m. basketball on sea
pilgrims of the dock	marseille	grooves of portcullis
pilgrims dock	dartmouth-plymouth	kittens smashing last nights last pint
pilgrims on the dock	leyden-delft haven	join (on) the docks

white stone towers, white-stone towering
soviet bleak concrete storeys tall
shivering everywhere to
you to hold, you to hold but

never sleep with anyone who has more scars than you

wanting to hold, you to hold but

only record, record this

a fucked-over kid, abused before they could name ... bright-eyed blonde
hooked on heroin and care, they traded you ... those liberal fuckers who
insist we are all captains of our ship ... freedom, oh aye, run to the wire
and fry, or at least to be shot as we try, to die on our feet, on our knees,
alone, together, singing ... to die revengeful, our fingers raised

pissing in sinks of whitestone bedsits is no life comrade, no life at all

held on, kept holding until your body wasn't, the blood-run cold ... guilty? most times i don't feel ... all their knowledge is pain, fighting together though no land was promised, d'ya have the right to deny their last, and it is their last wish? ... they tie off, tied off, the artery - needle - groove ... sick/ tired, all of it, of it all - your toytown lives, gilt-edge lies, gilded wives and taken down the docks, all the clichés, yeah, every

pissing in sinks of whitestone bedsits is no life comrade, no life at all

to race south, giving up everything, so lent - even though we are months out, and your tears in this last kiss, last kissing ever – not even the tick of wind, of gulls hawking, mast rattle carving you to bone ... wanting to hold you, wanting you to hold but, wanting to hold you, wanting you to hold but ... just a hulk other side the estuary and that ceaseless grey ebb flow ebb flow ebb

record this

record this

mind the reality gap

this is a whisper
from the kiss-off power elite

slipping her tongue in
knocking him off his feet

mind the gap

a hurricane of policies
rutting the night-flowering city

stand clear please

at their feet   a deregulated train
howling through ghost stations

we'd like to apologise

this is the nine o'clock rumors
spinning what might-of been

between the iron queen   and
her latest man in number ten

*

a couple play chess in the sun
they're both men

inside local gallery, depressives
spell *nuts* out their medications

and then to the bogs, the front
unable to crayon their swastikas right

i'm hard with memories of you
that motorway caff middle of the night

fuckwitted chants of *salman salman our son*
closing like your lips around my cock

*

lily white spray across glass
the model agency

but i'm inside station yeah
the head of steam yeah
conspiracies of coffee machines yeah

whispering
about me, us, him
all about love yeah
write me down yeah
write   me   down
elizabeth two   three
morning yeah
queens accepting business
cards store cards rent
cards visa delta
dining international
america repressed
masters switch/ed
even handful of my head
clipboards and chipboard
chips and billboards
cash we gotta have cash

thanks so much
thank you so much
so very much
thank you
thanks?
thanks anyway
you're welcome
sorry?

er, um, er, you know, well? er, um, er, you know, well!

11:07 /   11:07 / toilets on eight / 11:08 / 11:08 / platform
eight / 11:23 / 11:31 / 11:43

only thing missing is
how we have been made
to run on time, to run to time
say sorry sheetmetal maggie
powercontrol maggie
insert your coins now maggie
firework yobs clamp down pinochet flammables
duty is duty, schnapps is schnapps
... *this plague is sponsored by* ...
going crazy, am i? light up, two lads
reading fucksonnets blown out of pages
wave him aboard, giving red light to
trans pennine express

the four and a half inch heeldrag
the childkiller fuelband
the lifestyle, the rent
for real, cliff richard
way out, side gents
off platform eight
chippendales demolition
experts taking apart platform
beautiful man, oh it is yeah
d'ya like - nice? nice!
its best kids going cheap
over thousands of cliffs for rent
updown our sexyscampi
fully air conditioned
denimrub sheetmetal club

readers get naked
for the one-legged cliff
business suit cliff
helicopter pilot cliff
peeling paint off ladies
waiting no room
please shoot straight
please shoot   please

be their free god   bar none   just   two minutes   please

*

ravish the railworkers / cha-cha the miners - the firefighters /
rock the dockers / tango the fishermen the seamen the
cockworkers / nurse the healthworkers the stealthworkers
back to pain / with eyes like loaded exocets / her fierce
heterogaze / scudding the colonisation / that slaphappy
beautybitch / baroness thatcher / ramraiding the workers
rights / born again pay dash for colostomy cash / another
unskilled unnamed / eased off the jobless / greaselubed back
to work / so get it, get it out / this plague is sponsored by /
your liturgical meat godhead / this plague is sponsored by /
ethical cleansing is back again / whitenoise whitenoise
whitenoise / this plague is sponsored by / albion market nail
bombs whitemale bombs / wire coiled round her-his flower
death / gag the queeros / sweep the homeless off the street /
export all difference / viva la honest lie / this plague is
sponsored by / fisting slitwired mental debutantes / franchise
the working / the ünter classes / lasso the lasses / chain my
nipples up / we got cash-cow culture wanked over loony /
we got surveillance under threat / we got business as usual /
aye, we got business as usual

outstaring

to enter again the dance taking place, spilling out across
street, people weaving in out in, no-one touching but filling spaces we
leave behind, the cracked dance of our lives

i wear your concrete like a second skin england
outstaring shadows, pouring chips down throats
like lyrics to love-songs that you and god alone can hear
now shuffling feet - a sad little dance to the camera
now playing your tits out through the cold, the grey closing

pvc and plastic via your glass eye   apply for your security   pervert now
i'm the one you're staring at   apply for your security pervert now
you need to buy into my gloss   apply your pervert now
the s-s-s of seduction in my neck   apply please apply
you wouldn't know if i was in drag for now your pervert
                out   please now please
          and   now pervert security security security
             staring   and   and   and

maybe some nights i wanna cry
when you switch off
but your red eyes no gonna
no, you're never gonna catch that

the neural   darknesses unreal
the pathways   your coiled wire innards
the passage of   slow-fi red of night through low-fi lens
the have-a-go   you're seeing red as neon shifts up a gear
the jack the lad   daynight shifting to psycho
hero chic between the sheets analysis of
the sleek moves   zoom pan tilt   of in out in

outstaring your skinned desire rags of tinsel
your guitar suicide in e flat
your tequila and lime   this
spit skirts   the orbit
your hard rubber   of our drift and spin

snogging when you think no-ones watching   upside the concrete
slow wet tongue in   spying
when you know we are   in
persecuted   prosecuted   outstaring

the blackbox
eye
big
brother
scrawled
offbalance
to concretes
vertical
accompanying
red arrow
points
skyward
to slowsweep
recording
firstkiss
between
schoolkids
or pissing
in doorway
one drunk night
15 seconds
of fame
fingering   zoom pan tilt
fast-forward rewind   in out in
pausing over stop   all the lads the lasses love
on knocked-off videos   zoom pan tilt
of morningafter   in   out   in

i'd rather be shot by a camera
i'd rather be shot by a camera

i'd rather be shot

heart busting adrenalin
spot-lighting strip-teasing
neon corridor tunnelvision
night shivering pebble
-dash wood glass stone

your bones washed over   watched over
the mirrored eyeball bleed/s   frame by framed
tricks of lines closing in   oh baby   tracking you
on the blink   the neon city is tracking you

a slit of piss   peek-a-boo of wings stolen
the yellow spray   glass snatch and one way programmed
no flash please   but this little
no photography   pigged out in meatspace
no fucking way   and this little spied on your home

eye spy your cuppa tea   you're no my cuppa tea england

you're two spoons of sugar when mines a twist of lemon
and your yorkshire tea don't grow on the slopes of yorkshire

and your brands picked out   your eye in the sky   footsteps cracking
in the i.d. parade   all glazed apple camera cracked crazed
spinning discs   stuffed in gobs   glazed river
satelliting this world   gods drinking still   the mirror whistling
eyeing up   your air   your light i wanna
your stirring up another cuppa   wanna be
eye spy your theatre of the ordinary?

into the loop into the loop   cokelands fierce heterogaze queuing to
look 'em up   and down

all the in out in crowd   oh yeah   bird at reddening throat
                                     flutters
love a a a zoom   a moan
pan tilt a   a spit   oh god   a scream
lubricate quickening   oh   a calling out
a double yes   god   an ecstatic vision
any language   oh yeah

any tongue   oh   bright eyes
                                  oh   distortions
                           oh   through lives
all the in out in crowd   through-puts
love a a a zoom   oh god   yeah   the noise input
pan tilt a   a spit   the vertical
lubricate quickening   oh god   the horizontal
a double yes   oh   tracking lost
any language   yeah   the bent headset
any tongue   oh yeah   the manipulations of operators
                         oh god yeah

and its all done with mirrors - tricks of the / rear-view rearguard this is a
lifeguard situation / not repeat not / you've something of the light about
you / celluloid cellulose sell you the other / on the fake the take the razz
the make / confuse celluloid realities the real thing aint / wrap - the
ultimate wrap /what if only thing in our rear-view is mirror only, what if?

child mouths tomorrow is a photocopy of today

        addictive as porn you cannot stop looking
bride belting her groom with bunch of lilies

mean i'm doing the favour right, keeping my eyes / their denim - peeled

systems set, we wanna
we gonna, nail those
er um   er you know
nail your stuff
your live rhythm
your, you know
your thing, your
source of all
your ecstasy
paranoia, your
your oxygen
your mirror of desire
your mirror to desire
your thin mirror

gonna patrol, gonna petrol your
you're videoed, taped and tapped
wired for - ooh the cheats and slackers
move along now, lap it up, oh we like
wiped all the tapes, remote control
we are your, now turn over / up the tele
focus in, game yours, your silent game
turn yourselves in, gonna enjoy
and with eyes like that!   please help
secure the centre, peripheries
can go piss in the wind

england i wanna lie down your double yellows
stick my tongue through your tarmacademed cracks
and outstare until your insecurity cameras home to roost

england   i wear your concrete   a second skin

leery

you are now within a foot of the extreme edge

now is autumn
season of mists
and all that shite

day doesn't grow light
flame cracks the leaf
decay runs through

scraps of bin bags
on gulag wind
are hung on trees

prayer flags from
each small flat round my estate
calling for release

forecast is grey
the clag becoming critical
before dawn

as all this gravitates
toward axis of never-still world
don't fall asleep as child

this month
is a dusky moth
shot through with fire

poor perdu

lying on banks of that greened castle
we was kids in uniform
experimenting

touching your cracked lips
i tasted salt and blood
where his ringed fist had stung

tongue-dance - a saltarello
teasing back foreskin
of your taut cock

we rolled in mud   flattened grass
you came repeatedly
over face and hands and arse

later   i played the fool
called you my poor perdu
lost since the eighties

i believed in you
and then your family tree   your history
stared out from sunday papers

we are come to this great stage of fools

foreign heat beats on balding head
oxters heave and sweat

daddy leer topless   fist clenched
round home made pint of bulldog

this bleached beached leviathan
out back house bought from council

cheap cig between narrow lips
the accusing aperture starts

been so long since i settled their disputes
they used to   bring stuff too - eight-packs, fags

gross of lighters one time,
course i chucked the pink 'uns

back issues of fiesta, playboy
they paid me 'omage, they knew respect

lost ma kingdom when we moved
kept movin, ended in the cold north sea

came back again, knowin mine was
royal blood,   none that common red

mine was thick as thames passin parliament
heritage strong as albion hersel

tis the times plague, when madmen lead the blind

taking a break from
preaching life and crimes
down *king and country*
leery sits and shits
on his cracked throne
gut heaves, stains
porcelain to read
armi age sharks

when will man find peace
if no on the can
wean walks in
real cool i wipe arse
shove paper in her-twat-face
chrissst! who wouldn't
pay dear for
photo like that

courtiers float in pools
of piss-warm beer
last orders given
some bastard
drinking irish
flash of smash widens
smiling throat. *1-0, 1-0*
leery and the lads gloat

a disease that's in my flesh, which i must needs call mine

bleary guy
smelling of
piss and cig

splashes
sixteen quid
on tickets

crashes
a tenner
on instants

muttering
life's a lottery
of blood, sweat n bones

of televised trauma
n keepin
ahead of the jones

as he scratches
and tears
scratches and tears

double rollover
freezing
balls off

queuing out
reinforced
door   itching

to get fingers
burnt   as
mp's argue

when to trigger
cold weather
payments

then shall the realm of albion come to great confusion

hurricane tore through leers heartland

trees which stood before shakespeare are fallen
chaos from the butterfly who stomped her steel-capped boot
though thatchers heart was no longer in it

but still the greymen came   extending a decade of greed

smells of mortality

your carnivore belief in free market is now paid for
struck down through eating contaminated meat
half-blood cuts stolen from a pensioners picnic

ramble all you want, even your bladder bleeds and leaks
limp-dicked now daughters are grown, old man
no longer able to leer as they piss and shit, you are alone

you whoreson dog, you slave, you cur

hold ma fists   take ma cig
and brand your fuckin face
dinna need to spell hate
i have sticks, stones
rusty blades and broken bottles
and i can always throttle you

you'll no forget daddy leer
holdin court on his throne
what the fuck you needin
words for when fists'll fuckin do
but she had turned my folk sour
ma kingdom for a whore
stripped off ma fuckin back

get to fuck, out ma fuckin sight
hurled the whisky bottle
with all my fucking might
whore-son the lotta
vowed never let it
out control again, i'm
only executioner from now on

userer hangs the covener

electricity   gas   water   nuclear fools   road   rail
jails   airlines and the sky   owned 'em all

up and into wales and crossing reservoirs
i'm holding back billions of gallons

if i'd let go villages below would-of been washed away
piss a triumphal arch, good english cider bursting from vat

jets out training saluted me back, aye, i controlled it all
now i'm at her majesty's pleasure wondering what she'll make of me

we two alone will sing like birds i'the cage

swallow plucked midair
and dragged home by cat
i sang like her in your cage

called me flower never to be picked
said i was lady no like the others   until
you reached inside me smooth quim

as i passed round cheap beer
gave hard-slap, others spilt handful
of salted nuts and laugh it off

only i'd realised how to make you pay
oh da-ddee leery, flash my wee teets
or inch of gash, reach for your cash

groping round, fish out what i found
my prize - necklace or a fiver
more for two hands, nothing sordid mind

drawn to border marches, digging those
shifting wilder reaches of cliff top graves
skulls through whose sockets sand drifts

another hourglass running on empty
imagining the worms decades long
diet cutting you to the boner

now gods, stand up for bastards

hooded crow stares down with jet bead
the malignant eye piercing car-cass

wont shift until the last, this winged stone
rises cackling when brakes are hit

preacher, shaken, ministering to leery
candles so you're no in darkness

i'll pray for you and you can pray
i'm never caught, breakin such tender

flesh is the good lords work, my collar
openin doors, those sweet angelic whores

on bended knees after sunday schools
and church, bless, still protects me

i am a man, more sinned against, than sinning

hear me out
leery on his knees
cos of the old sow
you daren't cross
cold enough to trash bone
jeez mashed fist
against her brick
was in traction
half the week

pulled to sour teets
coarse hairs stinging
she don't care
seduced by the stare
she took leery's balls
foreskin ways back
teeth in hard and
cock-crown torn raggedy
giving her good laugh

cutpurse always wet
and stench to high
needing mask to go down
her pushing leery
head hurled below
into salt north sea
witchvoice screaming
you're no fuckin poof
are you ma son

tried showing her
with all the hate
he could muster
and pissing all over
her just laying there
enjoying gold shower
was then he swore
to master all
women like ma

the tempest in my mind,
doth from my senses take all feeling else

nagging wouldn't stop
should-of let me be
twenty runs short
one wicket in hand
overcast and black balls
like grenades at our
brave lads, swear i
forgot the can of lager

my bird just going over
frame by framed
bruise spreading slow
replays like childhoods
purple plums sweet oozing
and arse of maggot wriggling
like babby bird toppled from nest
your hands are too tight

and its no longer there
how it happened swear
still loved that old whore
though her teets was dry
couldn't stop weans crying
had to dip finger in my glass
and give sup until they curled
at peace to our stained floor

you gotta admire thatchers balls
really shook this cunt-ry up
and they says women
never declare war
built in ma's iron image
but it was us men
who welded 'em both
and us who put the rivets in

women will all turn monsters

didn't mind playing rough
long as it was fair
but your mates came to believe
you ruled, and you lorded it over
this parliament of fools until
nothing was tender any more

only patronage and fear
where once i wore veil for you
now a thin film of plastic
keeps fish from my hair
where you dropped me in concrete
baited hooks drift past my lips

one time piercing left nipple
the one you liked to sook
not the other   that one you bit
like a raging boar all tusk
i've lain long enough in deep water
maggots inquiring as to my health

one time sheep's carcass floated down
bumping into me and resting there
until explosion of meat
as some water-sport enthusiast
stuck his foot through our bloated bodies
- been so long since i last breathed

fie, foh and fum, i smell the blood

each day was guerrilla warfare
on knees in the playground of hate

teachers held mugs of sweet tea
looked on through reinforced glass

as my ribs cracked and perdu you pulled knife
forced 'em back   we talked of garrottes

cheesewire taut until tongues popped
lost child of albion shiny with tears

anthrax stains your crumbling core
we fucked in fields of blood and bone

now fertiliser is laced with paraffin
a fist of semtex in suburban litterbins

bomb dropped into cauldron of discontent
the co-ordinates on coded maps

are your streets and railway stations
your loved ones and your homes

black angel, i have no food for thee

leer killed ma
later he found another
and kicked me out

i journeyed wrong side of wire
visiting places
he could never even spell

only one place i wanted him
            hell
wishing the back of him

dark night rainy streets
us creeping on rubber
while his boots tick-a-tack-tick

nails sparking underfoot
creep close   strike hard
daddy-leer all mashed up

my dream for a decade
then over the water   smuggling arms
perfect   middle-englander

says so on passport
easing 'em across another's border
like greasing my lovers arse

hood down   gloves on
headlights killed   nosing around
only bombed my kind

my kin   theres no cowardice
in thrill of knowing
it could take you sky-high too

anti-terrors fucking animals
asked what i was up to other side
the water so much

said i was in love and showed hard cock
special branch squeezing my balls
i saw bright lights and fell

a flash of boot-tip leather
just like daddy-leer and just like him
they had to let me go

some say theres gonna be peace
again   i'll sit it out
someones always wanting

plastic explosives like a new life
to be pushed this way and that
like squeezing my lovers nipples

no sweat just hands like rock
concentrating on the fuse
ken who is other side this wall

get this one just right
i'm gonna take some lovers man
or sisters brother

i'm gonna take some babbies
bastard father tonight
they'll either thank or curse

makes no odds, do my job
laugh-fuck-cry
this ones for you daddy leer

when every case in law is right
and bawds and whores do churches build
then comes the time, who lives to see it

history's welt across your bloodied back
tattoo bearing imprint of memory
where once we spoke fairytales
revealed mask within the mask
retold a childs hood game

surviving beyond and
learning to stare unflinching
down barrel of camera
starved of all but bone-bleach sun
and hungering after

until all thats left becomes
charred page, crumble to ash
soaring on wind, erased in a single breath
i no longer remember how to cry said fool
into perfect morning after

but no-one was left to listen

honeysuckled

honeysuckles, honeysuckling, honeysuckled
city weeps honey, sweeps lines of light

tyne and tide unsleeping in writhe
great clots of soot and rivets untying eyes

in a game of hic-hac-hoc / paper-scissor ... whats
the chance on coming up stone each and every?

angels this north such a long time coming
where honeysuckles great-knot moors tower

caedmon bends to computer screen
her illuminated scream detonating night

up here where the smoke-damage dont,
star clusters spell out perfume time

slips out and at dawn tender-tendrils
alight to honeystone this city alone

foxes gloving it, their early
bells off - flay, fly and flee
home before sun-sups
and leaves of yggdrasil
pushing on up and thru
the drain main while

overhead, overheard
over wires, beneath bridges
dynamo-driven, light-riven
alive-arriving, electricitys
chatter-clatter stealing
a.m. eyes

      to power up laboratories
of spin and local par-liar-ments
breweries of light, libraries of neon
whole forests of tanning tubes
reefs of ice-cream generators
worker-toast, teas ringtones

will today bring winning numbers
or smoking outside the crem?

the sucked aching-teat overflow
and overflowering windows
new-stacked with
rib-trotter-shin

in this elec-tricked light
caedmon wanting to be
the words, the very words
so that breathed in, she
clothes kith and kin (in)
jeweleye, irepoint, ranter

blairs a fiver a go prossie
chalked down lawcourts
swiping cellophane wrapped
pack of carnations
rat-a-tat at mock
doric columns
flowerheads
rapid bulleting
their spray n pray
bites new paving hard
this shopped dummy
shine-white, tanned teeth
pulling off tee
breath suspends
from meat-hook
fists tattooed
black n white
eyes to gutter
horizons lowered
done and done in
and such displeasure
glass dark with
no remorse-code
neo labour or hard
modern blues all
one big con
- all thats on offer
is varying
percentages
of meat won
in local raffles

caedmon remembers jack common and how

*private enterprise secures maximum loss against one community or
another*

how she too wants to rip, revel and reveal

global warm strips out insulation
even the very name - cruddas park

rebranded riverside dene
when rivers an easy mile

arseholes sprayed around
the gare-casinos letterbox

and the exact time kit comes off
is widely advertised   caedmon

time-smeared, watching over
these dazed / hazed / lazed

their gold-keeper urging unleash
strike up the banned, strike for freedom

strike!   each girder and every -
a bloody yet crucial fiction

another back-end bus health campaign
two folks, hetero and white, but not too
ring-a-ring-a-rosying, till they all fall
but not too down, everyone singing
the tab divide, the perfect middle way
that line fine between responsibility
and rights - honeyed sweet nothings
of the con-dems when you come right down

                              - smokers die

buddleia coverts
its mauve dessert
in guttering, lags
around drainpipes
and culverts

red admirals
lighter and
later than
rolling papers

brighter than
vertical tanning
hook to this nectar

is more needed?

ribboning community orchards - they just might be : a
thousand and a thousand and a thousand bairns cherry-
stonings striping the c2c cycle-way, bloom breathed slender
and into fruitful reach - such is caedmons balm

her smile-lines are row upon row of garlic - chive - onion

and seedbombings till sore, nasturtiums - those sluts of the
plant world, are needed more than prow of new business
school; quinces more than executive offices; urging
honeysuckle more than the corporate codpiece - hostmens
approved public arts

and her laughter-linings silver as allotment found cutlery

a solace of urban meadow spreads before - marigolds /
oranges / coppers where houses have vacated elswick - and
within - caedmons tranced poppies deep, deeper, red reading
onto wind and rain and sun, her seed, her suck and her spore
- pasts yrs, futures ours

charcoal mostly
running outta dreams
cherry stones rain down
and theyre crying
whose lifted the onions
in summerhill square

for every alone they throw
caedmon gifts a piece skin
and bone, how quickly
honey-and-rose-stones grow

these honeysucklings
grin and all, s/hes been at
a millennium more and all
while tendrils climbing

mind is selling off cutlery
- knives are behind the counter
please ask

wrapper-upper ensures
bud vase for lover-sister-comrade
is padded to perfection

young goths
wearing their ribs on the outside
cry over onions in the gutter

pull wheelies
on borrowed wheelchairs
air-guitaring crutches

they couldnt be - well, less straight
like leazes park where the railing bends
surprised round that ash - tree of life

for these honey-slicked and licked
caedmon soft-slipper shuffles
translucent as vellum

last nights graff-writings rewiring

afraid the dada off wingrove road
love safe longing toward chinatown
lock&listen tagged round waterloo street
shock-crew alternates with *crazyfists*
angel with the raves on central payphones
kin-licit heading for the fake bridge while
renegade inches east on scratchy buses

plenty action and how now lawcourts
downing shutters, so that on and over
rosed-stone and polished railings
parkouristas make the running, all the
run-wheel drop-jumping, rare-lazy
into reverse and vault-climb-spiral
their art displacing concrete for moments
at a time, tearing cat-balances and un-
          thru to bodymind swimming-air

tee-shirts read *make parkour not law*

old football pitch of arthurs hill and dropped cd *now thats
what i call* ... vol 68 and for encore discarded *clockwork
orange* dvd frisbee'd against the drear for a rescued mastiff

wouldnt under the beach, the pavement be more like?
caedmons suckle, future-plant castling to rerun repeat
retread, these times she forgets to remember, her flesh
mobbing

ice-cream chiming
and the goalie chanting
take me to the place
take me to the place

this age is hard to tell
gender apart, their kissings
yuuuuu baaad bastarrrd
ooh you baad

back-to-backs fat with light
roses-just-hipped
lanterning to ground
mams calling 'em home

and the kissing bairns
hold tongues in reserve
the land asbo forgot - for now
and caedmon never will

seasons new jackdawing
to parkouristas very move wheeling air-spin
hunt late bugs / grubs, rejecting greggs seconds
stalemating around pill court, refusing even freegan
end-of-days - crayfish sandwiches with artisan cress
- excess the soup kitchen barely stomachs

pasties pigeon-bombed into vault spiral
swift break out-climb wheel crash-tag
branches just-turned leaves a-shaking
only for gulls to close - bursting
on thru in hardcore pastie fight

jackdaw-wing foliaged for the wee greens
those bugs, grubs, chrysalises tree'd

in a knuckle-crack
starlings marrack
vent wheel
and again
cherrys morello
to beak
all raining
in
  on
    down
leaf tear this
share-crop
conch of bark
sounding
lope
  lop
    hawk
on shuffle repeat
their bust
raking this
late cherry then
massive off-swerve
as one feather
to the roosting

caedmon brushing at eyelash that wont, just wont fall

the unlucky who - meaning it ironic -
told her approved social worker to *run with it*
just as they scissored out her blisterpacked meds

now repetitively stubbing flesh out and outside
        the new deal fire-station where bhangra lads
hang u-turns - england air-fresheners off rear-views

vendors of porn wishing each and every *lu-uverly day*
earl grey whose catch-and-only phrase *shit on me?*
ex chief-whip signing off in a crayon of rainbows

whose fuelling and who aint? who's duel is it?
whose singing they regret near enough everything?
the urge to get torn not worn in this strange refuge
disconsolate bairns - caedmon drip bleeds still
her futures building ideas and ideals

against deniers of difference in their d.i.y. panopticon-and-on - the city might not burn but wheelie-bins do, silver birches burnings and bongs burnt-out as are sunderland tops and refugees welcome - all fanning gangbangers of self-appointed hate. but antifa, their stickers fighting back against the fascists and lamposting caedmons estates; plus, the mela recently stormed with roaring drums - handy lads and lasses promising in fire-fight; and fenhams cardamom barfi, besan laddoo and halwa, indian sweets as kite-scraps of beauty - hate cannot mask this coral and coralled, this reef of tyneside international - outerground gritstone and true, aye, caedmons nosegays all. always remember honeys the fist that sticks. how her honey is the fist that sticks. treacling gloops of light stealing on down - the streaked jewels forging magpies nest, this toon where caedmon north-moved and first awakened honeysuckle to climb thru nights, its perfumery booming great aching swathes and swags

drinks can blown up pitt street, blows on up sheer in vent
bairns of the homeless dropping their cheese-string
watch as fluorescent marker stamped throb-pink to retro
cobbles clipclopping one of poundworlds plaster saints
clip-clop ace of spades, joker in the gutter long blown
cli-cli-clop aftershock shots glass rolling idly wild
pair of police horses stride-striving for canter
no longer the happy plod but shucking off
their heavies, trot and gavotte not garotte
anarchy horses infiltrate ex-breweries
- to these ribald piebalds, caedmon
hymning them emma goldmans
whats the point of revolutions
unless you can dance
permanently

c.p.n. signed off and queuing for spring rolls and broken dreams
fire-fighter in designer glasses waiting on beef and broken promises
jack common queuing for sweet&sour and false-dawns
bea campbell queueing for good szechuan sauce
kurt schwitters quiet immersion in bamboo shoot
charmers and charvas, bruises and bruisings
sucklers and sucklings, mama-san, her wok
- an impossible great mobius, never running dry
like the grand river itself, she feeds them all

and all the while mama-san sings
peppers are red, the peppers are red
the peppers are red and yellow
the peppers are red and yellow
and orange and green but mostly
red, aye - the peppers are red

            delicately stir-frying
pak-choi in oyster sauce
caedmon has this
dribbling her chin
and how!

tyres ringing the queer quarter
mouth surprised o's, this grunge halo
no lipstick / lipslick, slid-quick, lip now hip
quip whole other continents, tongues, throats

gay hadrian and that imperial peace-keeping
right-angles and straight straight lines?

                                        postcard home
                                    - this westgate road
has turned queer - halal-tool-hire-ink-refills;
tho white beer, imported figs, tanning
- those the emperor understands

fag-end firefly sparks
afterlight / afterdark
arcwelds fragile
bridging which gap
breathing frail skin
exact weight of
cigarette papers
before the inhalation

the flicker of faces
the flicking of v's
salt before crash
escape mirror-glass
a city on the move
near-continuous
rebuild-rebrand-re
... pace hard
to upkeep, plus
the noise of this!

militant in her
redrawings
redoublings
fractal-sing
caedmons got
this licked, aye
all the new
grotesqueries

romans guarding pons aelius, anglo-saxon monkchester,
caedmons professional northerner then scribed early verse -
visioning and moving north to normans destruction
rebirthing novum castellums most northern fortress -
caedmon too losing her unwanted length, lop-chopped a swell
unselling honeysuckle-honeysuckled-honeysuckling to
provide the honeystone and the rose-stone thru border wars,
reivers, hostmen, keels and keening, scots parliamentarians
keeping king this not so new-castle, face peels are nothing
new, dont need tanning, await late summers early dew,
caedmon aye licking the fallen blue star, their gare-staring-
wound, lick the woundering to clot, bairns by scruff, caedmon
is her own crew

..... these nights are they practising fun or practised emergencies?
rednose beside metro track, some joker to pocket alongside cable
whiteface blown into high branches a bleached carrierbag
jacket left for the riverside rust-deer graze and gazing
trews hung in the honeycombings of seven stories
boots ascend the civic bell-tower, the slowdrip
nursery rhyming, cradle, cradle, cradle
rock and bye, rock and bye
rock and bye .....

and breathe in the moth-sky and sly wolf-light messages seeping night-time libraries, saints and swingers cemeteries, frying bread and fried pans, improvising bridges, kittiwakes feedbacking, drivers cutting up casualty, the casual *stitch that*, tracks and track-marks, walls and wallflowerings. so many honey-bound wounds, such sweet-amber blastings, such a lotta anarchy-laughings. caedmon is her own marginalia unmooring from pages this great illuminated, like corporation seahorses upping anchor and floating free, the apocrypha of millennias merging, smile lines from corners her mouth are girders webbing; her onion skin sloughs off, sloughs off, great crack-winged manuscripting in flight, her honeysuckle-honeysuckling-honeysuckled of pre-dawn and the fist that will always stick, clothing each and every, beautifully with jeweleye, irepoint, ranter